God, Guns, Grits, *and* Gravy

A Satire

God, Guns, Grits, *and* Gravy

A Satire

Mike Huckleberry

2014

New Street Communications, LLC

Wickford, RI

About the Cover Artist

Stanko's paintings have been exhibited throughout the tri-state area, including shows at the prestigious Elaine Benson Gallery in Bridgehampton and the Empire State Building. He has been interviewed numerous times on television and has donated his artwork to many causes over the years such as breast cancer walks, Art for ALS, and The Waterkeeper Alliance, to name a few. Stanko, a lifelong native of Long Island, is represented by The Ripe Art Gallery in Huntington, New York. For more information: *stankoart.com*.

I awoke one morning to a country I no longer recognized. I mean this figuratively, of course; I'm not senile. I was clearly still in the United States of America, in the master bedroom of my sprawling Florida estate. A cool breeze lifted the lace window curtains in lazy gusts.

But that day something in the air was different.

Something was rotten.

I raised the sheets to check my adult diaper, reassured to find I was not the source of the corruption.

But what was it then?

I turned on the bedroom television only to be confronted by an openly gay news anchor, his wedding ring gleaming in the studio lights. He was rambling on about the "unequal" policing of African American communities and the "militarization" of law enforcement, whatever that means. Our illegitimate President was to have a press conference at two PM. This was followed by a commercial conducted almost entirely in Spanish.

I rubbed my temples, having suddenly developed a throbbing headache.

What was different? America was turning into an open sewer of liberal diarrhea. And it stank, by God, it stank to high heaven.

Where had we gone wrong? I wondered. When had the Godly, righteous voices of truth and conscience succumbed to the whisperings of Satan?

It seemed the road to hell was paved in rationalizations.

Why shouldn't gay couples be able to marry? It's love.

Minority communities ought to have equal representation on police forces and in local government. Qualifications be damned.

Let's just throw a welcome mat down on the southern border. We're America—diversity is our thing.

I was roused from my thoughts by the sound of childish laughter emanating from outside the house, coming up the drive.

Sliding my Bushmaster out from beneath the bed, I crept on all fours toward the window, preparing myself for whatever lay beyond. Gathering my nerve I peeked through the curtains, and surely enough, winding their way up the driveway was a group of Girl Scouts, a pair of female chaperones trailing behind them—holding hands.

"My God," I whispered, switching the safety off my weapon. They were ringing the doorbell then, and as they did so I slid on my belly like a serpent onto the sun-warmed balcony.

These monsters weren't selling cookies or collecting cans, no—their agenda was far more insidious in nature. They were peddling pro-choice, socialist, homosexual, leftist propaganda wrapped in neat little khaki packages.

I popped up like a Viet-Cong sniper, aiming my assault rifle at the degenerates.

"All right ladies!" I shouted. "Fun's over! Run on back to the Planned Parenthood center!"

"We're selling cookies!" the littlest of the girls announced, at which point I shot the box of coconut shortbread out of her hands.

She screamed and began to flee along with the rest of them, waving their arms, tears streaming down their faces.

"We're not buying, commies!" I laughed, emptying my weapon into the air as they disappeared down the drive.

I went downstairs to where a breakfast buffet had been laid out, my black manservant George greeting me.

"Good morning, Governor Huckle—"

I backhanded him across the face.

"Damn it, George! How did those trespassers make it onto the grounds?"

3

"I'm not in charge of security, sir," he whimpered, rubbing his cheek.

"Always an excuse with you people, isn't it? Where's my paper?"

He swallowed hard. "The boy didn't deliver it today. I'd be happy to run out and grab a copy if you want."

"George," I said quietly, restraining my anger, "you've worked here a long time, but so help me God, if you *ever* take such an uppity tone with me again I will blast you out of this house with a fire hose. You get me, spooky?"

"Ye-ye-ye-yes sir," he stammered, turning to prepare my plate.

I took my breakfast on the shaded patio, reviewing the events of the morning while George sanded down my bunions.

What sort of country had this become when a man could be attacked in his own home by a troop of bloodthirsty communist Girl Scouts? And more importantly: if this liberal aggression were to go unchecked, unchallenged, what would come next?

I was glad Janice wasn't alive to see it. My wife had been killed eight years earlier, struck by a bolt of lightning at a Christian rock festival.

She'd been spared this downturn in American culture, and in that sense she was fortunate.

We'd grown up in a different America; a more wholesome

America. Why, my father used to make me chop a cord of wood for every extra minute I spent in the bathroom—two minutes being his strict limit.

"We know what you're doing in there!" he would shout, summoning my mother to stand with him outside the door. "You can't hide from God, Michael!"

"I'm going poop!" I would cry, forcing. "I'm going as fast as I can, I swear!"

And they would start banging on the door, chanting: "Mikey's going to hell! Mikey's going to hell!"

I became addicted to laxatives as a result, but I maintain to this day that it made me a stronger man. Yes, I've been in adult diapers since I was thirty due to the irreparable damage to my colon and sphincter, and I'm liable to shit myself if I sneeze too hard, but that's a small price to pay for a strong character.

Still, somewhere along the line the American dream had turned sour. We the people had fallen short of our promise, neglected our duty as God's chosen people—that shining city on a hill—guiding light to the rest of the world.

But we were not too far-gone. Not by any means.

A strong, decisive leader was needed, one with a close relationship to God; a man of principle, who could restore integrity to our great nation.

It was then that I had an epiphany.

"George," I shouted, startling him, "take dictation! I'm having a spiritual vision!"

In a second he was by my side with a pen and paper. "When you're ready, Governor."

It poured from me like a great fount.

"A national tour of epic proportions, to touch the heart of America—the true, God-fearing heart of America! I want to meet steel workers and coal miners and border guards and policemen and firemen! I want controlled, carefully orchestrated events with well groomed, well spoken minorities! I want babies and puppies and kittens, cows and screeching eagles! I want a commercial where I chase an immigrant family back across the border with a spear-tipped American flag pole!"

George scribbled frantically, trying to keep up.

"I want Huckleberry signs running off into the sunset with catchy slogans! I want a picture of me shooting fireballs from my eyes into IRS headquarters! YES! Are you getting all this?! I feel as if God has reached into my skull! I am a mouthpiece of the Lord, George!"

He nodded enthusiastically. "Yes sir."

"Don't sass me, George! I warned you about that! Now where was I?! Oh yes! Takers! 'Takers Beware' posters! And Muslims! Billboards of me boxing Muhammad—a still frame of me landing a knockout punch, mouth-guard flying with a spray of sweat and saliva!"

"Sir, I don't know if that's—"

"Don't interrupt me, George! You'll disrupt my connection with the Godhead!"

He shut up, letting me roll on.

"It's all so clear now! Only *I* can save the American people!" I leapt up from my chair, spreading my arms wide. "This is a truly momentous day," I whispered, tears welling in my eyes.

And so it was that I, Michael Dale Huckleberry, former Governor of Arkansas, Baptist Minister of twelve years, noted author, lecturer and political commentator, would run for President of the United Sates.

There was so much to be done.

But there was someone I had to see first.

"Back in my day we didn't call it the shocker," my father spoke, extending his index, middle, and pinky fingers in a shriveled, liver spotted claw. "No sir, we called it the James Brandelson, after the man who invented it. 'Give her the old James Brandelson' I used to say. 'Works every time.'"

"Dad, do you have to be so crude?"

My father, who recently celebrated his hundredth birthday, no longer seems to recall the fact that he was a devout Christian and an upstanding member of our community. What he does seem to recall however is a secret life of debauched sexual escapades he kept hidden from my mother and I.

He now feels it necessary to share every sordid detail of that life with the nearest passerby.

"—and it got so I just couldn't finish unless I had that damn butt-plug in."

"Good God, Dad! Could you stop it for just two minutes? I want to tell you about my new campaign. I'm going to be President, Dad." I smiled, taking his hand.

He looked at me with something akin to pride, and I felt my heart flutter. Was this the approval I'd sought from him my entire life? Finally?

He motioned for me to move in closer, so I did.

"I should have pulled out and spurted you onto that cheap hotel bed spread, you troglodyte. You're the worst thing that ever happened to me."

"God knows you don't mean that, Dad."

"There is no God," he said, quite matter of factly.

"Yes there is!" I shouted. "There *is* a God and *he* made me! Not you, you cankerous old fart! He made me for great things! Miraculous things! I'll show you!"

"GOOD! Show yourself the door first, you sniveling shit!"

I stormed out, sobbing.

I would show him. I would show them all.

"Praise the Lord," I whispered as Fox News's Megyn K—announced the Supreme Court's decision on Burwell v. Hobby Lobby, setting women's rights back at least a hundred years. "God's will be done."

"Choke on that one, King Obama!" Nick Fulton shouted, popping open a bottle of champagne as our plane bounced through a small pocket of turbulence.

Nick was my Chief of Staff as Governor and before that he was one hell of a campaign manager, so when I mentioned the possibility of a presidential bid, he jumped at the opportunity.

"We couldn't have timed it better, sir," he said, handing me a flute of champagne, "such a positive note to begin the tour on. Tangible evidence that the conservative, independent spirit of the nation is alive and well—rampant in fact!"

The plane buckled again.

"Have we decided on a first stop, Nick?"

"Dunkerton, Iowa. There's a CCA gathering and they're very excited to have you."

"Ah, the Christian Coalition of America. Good God fearing folks. Bless their hearts."

"Should we get back to work on your candidacy speech, sir?"

"Yes, let's do that. Take dictation, Nick."

He took out a pad and paper.

"Good evening, my fellow Americans," I began. "That our nation is in a state of decline is not up for debate. We're headed downhill faster than a shopping cart full of bricks—only our shopping cart is full of aborted babies, drugs, and social deviants."

"That's a very nice touch, sir."

"Thank you, Nick," I said, continuing on. "Now, white guilt may have elected Barack Hussein Obama twice, but we now know that experiment to be a monumental failure of both domestic and foreign policy."

"Gotta have the white guilt in there," Nick said, nodding.

"Indeed," I agreed. "The middle class is struggling in an increasingly uncertain economic environment, and for the first time in decades the next generation is expected to be less successful than the previous."

"Definitely need to frighten people."

"You bet your ass... Now apathy is rampant among our youth, and they are succumbing to the lure of drugs and premarital sex to fill their spiritual voids."

"Gotta have the premarital sex."

"Damn right... The scourge of liberalism has created a moral vacuum in which tabooed behaviors have become fashionable."

"Scourge of liberalism—love it, sir."

"Homosexuals flaunt their sinful lifestyles with pride in the media and on our streets. Men are becoming women, and women men. The nuclear family has mutated beyond all recognition."

"Excellent, sir. Always bring it back to the family."

"When you go to use an ATM you're forced to choose between English and Spanish languages. Illegal immigrants are surging across our southern border like a Biblical plague."

"Xenophobia's the ticket. You're on a roll now, sir."

"America is less respected in the world today than at any point in our history, even among our own population!"

"Morale is certainly low," Nick said, nodding.

"Well, ladies and gentlemen, it is my intention to right the course of our mighty vessel, and therefore I wish to announce my candidacy for President of the United States. I ask to be your shepherd in this time of darkness, and to guide you, by the grace of God, into a bright and prosperous future. A future we can look forward to.

"May God bless you, and may God bless the United States of America. Thank you and goodnight."

Nick stood and began a slow clap.

"Welcome to Dunkerton!" Mayor Dick Tucker exclaimed, shaking my hand. "It is a real honor to have you here, Governor Huckleberry."

"Well it's great to be here in your fine town," I said. "I take it you're a member of the CCA?"

"Lord yes," he said, wiping his sweaty bald head with a handkerchief. "I'm not in costume though. That wouldn't be appropriate given my position as an elected official, but the others have gone all out for today, believe you me."

He laughed, and I laughed along with him, not understanding.

"I'm sorry, did you say costume?"

"Yes," he laughed, "I can't be Dickey the Clown and Mayor of Dunkerton at the same time, now can I?"

"I'm not following."

He looked at me queerly.

"Well you're here to speak for the CCA event, right?"

"Yes," I said, "the Christian Coalition of America."

He shook his head.

"Nope. No sir, this here is a gathering of the Conservative Clowns of America. Hell, Dunkerton is only the clown capital of the world."

We rounded a corner onto Main Street where we were confronted by at least seven-hundred clowns who all turned in unison. Their red painted mouths stood in livid contrast with their pale white faces, lips twisted up in hideous, contorted grins.

The blood drained from my face.

Nick was quick to my side, whispering in my ear.

"Those are conservative votes, Governor. That's all you need to think about."

"Have you ever seen so many in broad daylight? It's like a nightmare."

"We shouldn't keep them waiting, sir." He motioned to the television crews that were set up nearby.

"Nick, I've never felt the need to share this with you until just now, but I have a deep-seated fear of clowns."

He pulled me in close, adjusting my tie.

"Just think of them as God's children, sir."

"God's got nothing to do with them," I said, panicking. "Look at their mouths. They look like they've been gorging themselves on blood."

"Well maybe they have been. Liberal blood! If you want to see them as monsters, that's fine. But they're your monsters, sir. They're in your corner. Just keep that in mind."

"I guess it's not so bad, if you put it that way—"

"That's the spirit," he said, pushing me forward, at which point the crowd erupted with shrill, demented laughter and honking horns.

A sea of white-gloved hands enveloped me, and I thanked God for that small mercy; if one had touched me with bare skin I think I would have lost my mind.

Those high voices—it gives me chills to think of them even now.

"Hellooooooo Governor Huckleberrrrrry!"

"I read alllllllll of your boooooooks!"

"Would you sign my whoopeeeeee cushion?!"

"Squeeeeeeze my nose! DO IT!"

Finally I reached a podium, which was covered in balloon animals, confetti and streamers, and tapped the microphone to test it.

"Would you care for some helium?" Mayor Tucker asked, offering me a balloon.

"I'll pass, thanks," I said. "I'm a real lightweight."

He laughed, throwing back his head and holding his sides. "We've got a joker here! I love it!"

The motley crowd erupted again in deranged laughter.

"Thank you, thank you," I spoke, raising my hands to quiet them. "Ladies, gentlemen, it's truly an honor to be here with you toda—"

"GET THAT CHOCOLATE MAN OUT THE WHITE HOUSE!" a purple-haired clown shrieked, the rest of them roaring in agreement.

"Good sir," I said, addressing him, "I can't speak as to whether or not the President is in fact made out of chocolate. I won't say that he isn't, because truthfully I don't know—I'm not a scientist. But I submit to you that any six foot tall chocolate confection endowed with the ability to speak and parading around under the name Barack Hussein Obama would most certainly be a hand puppet of Satan!"

The clowns screeched in approval.

Back on the plane Nick set a glass of scotch in my hand.

"I think that went fairly well, sir. All things considered."

I looked at him wearily.

"I'm glad you think so, Nick."

"Governor," Nick said, flipping his phone closed, the world whipping past us through the limo's tinted windows. "Something's happened."

"Well, what is it?" I asked, closing my Bible on my *What Would Jesus Do?* bookmark.

"It's Pastor James R—, sir. He's passed away."

"Good Lord! When? What happened?"

"He was found dead of an apparent heart attack this morning—"

"God rest his soul. My first job was working for him in Christian broadcasting. If ever there was a good, kind hearted—"

"Sir, he was found in a sex harness, a full-body leather bondage suit, ball gagged with a dildo up his ass... A 'Black Marauder' according to the police report... An underage Asian male prostitute was found unconscious in an adjoining room... There was

18

significant evidence of hard drug use."

"But—But—"

"Sir, we need to get a statement out ahead of the news cycle. We need to put as much daylight between you and the Pastor as possible."

"I don't believe this! When did they turn him?"

"Who, sir?"

"The gays of course! How did they get to him?"

"You're thinking of vampires, sir. That's not how it—"

"You seem awfully familiar with their practices!"

"No, sir. I just—"

"Silence!" I shouted, massaging my temples. "I need to think."

I looked out my window at a passing billboard. It was for a large jewelry chain, the ad featuring a well dressed handsome young man proposing to another well dressed handsome young man.

I vomited down the front of my suit.

Nick moved to help clean up the mess.

"No," I said, raising a hand, still staring out the window. "Let me just sit in it for a while."

"I understand the pressures young people face these days," I said, addressing the anti-drug rally. "By God, even our current 'President' is a burnout. I'm not sure that a former member of the Choom Gang is a suitable role model for our youth, if you know what I mean. What with the smokin' and the snortin' and the poppin' and the droppin', and God knows what else."

Laughter rippled through the crowd.

I took a sip of water from the cup that had been set out for me. It had a slightly bitter, alkaline taste to it that lingered on my tongue, but I was parched and so downed the rest of the cup.

"But seriously," I continued, "I am personally familiar with the horrors of drug abuse, as I myself was in the grips of laxative addiction for twelve years. Now that's not an easy thing to admit, but it is a part of who I am. I accept it."

The crowd clapped in support.

"Thank you, thank you," I said, tearing up a bit.

My speech was to go on for about an hour, and it was into the fourth quarter of that hour that I began to feel a bit odd. It was just little things at first. Somehow I felt lighter than usual, and the day had become strangely brighter, more vivid. I attributed these effects to having gotten a little too much sun, and decided to continue on.

I was then struck suddenly by the impression that I was impossibly tall, the ground seemingly hundreds of feet below me. I was at once amused and horrified by this, gripping the podium, my hands feeling sweaty and somewhat alien.

A shiver shot up my spine, sending electric waves rippling through my body, nerve endings igniting like Fourth of July fireworks.

I looked up to see that the standing audience had merged into a sea of undulating colors, surging, mounting before me like a looming Tsunami.

"Please don't!" I shouted into the microphone, the feedback shrieking like a thousand eagles.

I looked skyward to see a hummingbird dart by, leaving a streaming trail of blue green tracers in its wake.

The limbs of nearby trees had begun to slither and writhe like tentacles against the clear blue of the cloudless sky, through which swirling, breathing patterns had begun to express themselves.

21

Nick was by my side then, his face like some awful Halloween mask, loose and slick looking.

"Sir," he spoke, tongue flicking like a serpent's. "Are you all right, sir? You're very pale."

"Nick, I think I'm losing my mind," I slurred, the words seeming to bubble from my mouth.

"Let's get you out of here, sir," he hissed, his features turning reptilian as he guided me down off the stage.

Hands were reaching for me from all sides as we moved through the crowd, and I had the distinct impression that they wanted to tear me limb from limb.

A hideous child grinned up at me with a face full of razor sharp teeth. He lunged forward, hugging me about the waist, his monstrous parents clapping and guffawing, pointing a camera at us.

"Smile now, don't pout," is what they said, but what I heard was: "Pull his eyes out."

I screamed, wriggling out of the boy's grip, Nick pushing me onward.

The crowd parted ahead of us and belched forth a figure with an enormous paper mache Obama head, glittering marijuana leaves for eyes, grinning like a demon from the depths of the Dark Continent.

I fainted at the sight.

"What's that, Lord? I'm sorry, I didn't catch that."

Jesus leaned in closer. "I said you look very handsome today, Mike."

"Oh," I said, running my hands over my suit. "You are too kind, Lord."

The hallucinogenic concoction I'd been dosed with at the anti-drug rally turned out to be of a highly potent variety, and had provided such a shock to my nervous system that I was now in a direct line of communication with our Lord and Savior. Now while a normal person might see fit to seek psychiatric help for such a thing, I simply accepted it as a miracle. Jesus made me promise not to reveal his presence to anyone, however. He said they wouldn't understand, and who was I to argue with the son of God?

The door to the dressing room opened, Nick stepping in.

"Who were you speaking to just now, sir?"

"Oh no one," I said, throwing Jesus a wink.

He gave me two thumbs up in return.

Nick eyed me curiously as I made my way past him.

"What's the crowd like?" I asked. "Seem in a good mood?"

"It's a Catholic Elementary School, sir. I imagine it'll be pretty softball."

"All right," I said, straightening my tie. "Let's turn on the charm."

The Principal was still addressing the kids.

"And now, without further ado, it is my distinct pleasure to introduce the former governor of Arkansas, Mike Huckleberry!"

I walked out to loud applause, shook the man's hand, and stepped up to the podium.

"Thank you St. Peter's Elementary for inviting me here today. It's always wonderful to meet such promising, intelligent young citizens, and I can't tell you how pleased I am to be here. I think we're going to have a lot of fun."

More applause.

"Now," I said, "why don't we start with a few questions just to warm up. Just raise your hand and I'll point to you and someone will pass a microphone."

Many hands shot up.

"Oh my, lots of inquisitive young minds here. How wonderful. How about you there, little girl in the front row."

A microphone was passed to the little blonde girl.

"Why don't you tell us your name, sweetie?"

"My name's Molly," she said.

"Molly, well isn't that a lovely name. And what is your question, Molly?"

She took a deep breath. "As a Republican, what alternative policy would you pursue with regard to the millions of previously uninsured people who gained health coverage under the Affordable Care Act? Or do they not count as people?"

Off stage both Jesus and Nick face palmed themselves in unison.

I laughed nervously.

"Oh my, that's a mighty big question for such a little girl... Well, what you need to understand is that Obamacare is hurting the economy—"

"But that's not borne out by the statistics," she interrupted. "You just keep saying that over and over again. The most recent CBO report clearly indicates that—"

"Ok Molly," I cut her off. "Thank you so much for your thoughtful question!"

There was a brief round of applause.

"Now let's see here, who else has a question?"

A young African American boy raised his hand.

"You there, what's your name son?"

"Anthony," he said, taking up the mic.

"And what's your question, Anthony?"

"Where does the right wing media get off suggesting we're living in a post-racial society when it is in fact conservatives themselves who are trying to suppress the vote in communities of color? Isn't this indicative of the right's continued portrayal of non-whites as 'other'?"

"That's simply not the case, young man. You've been misinformed. We are the party of Lincoln, after all."

"Sir," the boy sighed, "with all due respect, you're a hell of a long way from the party of Lincoln."

"Ok," I said, "moving on."

I searched desperately for the least intelligent looking child I could find.

"Yes, you there," I pointed, "with the obvious Down syndrome."

The boy stood, accepting the microphone, and then quite eloquently inquired about my policy concerning the Middle East given the rise of sectarian violence and the destabilization of the Syria-Iraq border.

I mulled the question over briefly, then dropped the microphone and ran.

"Facing the Future. *Facing* the Future, for the love of God!" I shouted, holding up one of the tens of thousands of signs that were being distributed across the country at that very moment.

My likeness stared back at me, eyes bright with hope, wrapped in an American flag and cradling a Bible, beside the bold words proclaiming:

Mike Huckleberry for President.
Fucking the Future.

"Heads will roll for this, Governor. I assure you," Nick said. "But on a positive note, sir, the youth vote loves a candidate with a sense of humor."

"Don't give me that horseshit!" I gasped, hyperventilating.

"Well, we can always play it off as liberal sabotage."

I nodded, sliding down the hotel room wall, breathing heavily into a paper bag.

"It ain't been easy, Governor, let me tell you," Emmett de Beaufort spoke, his course voice cutting through the humid Louisiana night air. "I knocked up my second cousin a couple months back, which is funny because I thought I was sterile from working at the chemical plant. Damn thing's gonna come out with flippers, but what can you do—every life is sacred... After that I accidently shot myself in the foot out hunting. Was drunk, you see. Anyway, week after that my best bloodhound got run over by a busload of beaners gettin' shipped up north from the border, and then to top it all off the law come in and busted my kid for cookin' meth outta his camper. Fuckin' Nazis... But look at me rambling on when you ain't even got a piece of coyote yet. How do you take it, Gov? Look like a rare man to me."

"Right you are, Emmett," I said, grimacing as I forced down a swig of moonshine. "And thank you again for hosting this. Don't get out to many good old fashioned barbeques these days."

"My pleasure, Governor. It's just how we do. When we heard you was coming through, the whole community just pulled together. Gonna send you up to Washington, boy. Straighten those nigger lovin' commies right the fuck out."

"Couldn't have put it more eloquently myself, Emmett."

I looked over beside the row of trailers to where a fire had been laid. Atop it stood an effigy of Barack Obama, nailed to a cross, a Burger King crown set upon his head. The smell of kerosene permeated the area.

"Very lifelike," I commented.

"Thanks Governor," Emmett replied, handing me a plate of rare coyote. "The kids have been working on it for weeks. Gonna fire the little African prince up after supper."

Jesus was by my side then, pointing to the plate.

"Do you think I could get a piece of that?" he asked. "I'm starving."

"Ted C— would like to schedule a photo op with you, Governor," Nick said from my hotel room doorway.

"You tell that greasy-haired, McCarthy look-alike, Dr. Seuss readin' dandy that I'll do a photo op with him the day Ronald Reagan rises from the grave and starts twerking to Miley Cyrus."

"That's a no then?"

"Of course not! Cross Ted C—? My God! The Tea Party would eat me alive! Why don't I just blow my brains out?!"

"How's Tuesday for you?"

"Tuesday's no good. John M— and I are shooting an adult diaper commercial together. Gotta keep those living skeletons coming out to the ballot box. Wheel out the vote, you know."

"Very good, sir."

"That good God-fearing Christians should be persecuted for believing in the sanctity of marriage of all things is unbelievable. And when I say marriage I mean marriage in its one true acceptable form—one man, one woman, and a lifetime of bitter disappointment and lowered expectations!"

The Faith and Freedom conference erupted in applause.

"The family unit is sacred, and who are *they*—atheists, sodomites, lesbians, trans-gender pedophile deviants—to dictate to us the definition of the modern family?! There is but one family—one capable of natural procreation! No surrogate mothers for gays, no artificial inseminations for lesbians, only natural, heterosexual reproduction. If I am elected President, my first order of business will be to enact a federal ban on same sex adoptions. I will also be crafting legislation to bar these deviants from working anywhere near schools!"

Applause sounded again, but as it slowly died down a voice came through the crowd.

"Oh Daddy, still such a bitch!"

No God, I thought. *Please no.*

But yes, it was *him.*

Sauntering down the aisle with his gelled hair, his cut-off t-shirt revealing his toned abs and pierced belly button, his designer jeans seeming two sizes too small, lisping all the way.

"Daddy," he said, taking off his sparkly sunglasses to reveal mascara caked eyes. "You must stop all this craziness, Daddy!"

"I don't know you," I shouted. "Security! Security, remove this man!"

But they were nowhere to be seen.

"What?" he shouted. "You don't recognize your only son?!"

Gasps broke from the audience.

"It's not true!" I cried.

"Oh, it's true!" he continued. "Though you weren't man enough to come to my wedding—which was lovely, by the way. Manuel says 'hi'. We enjoyed the fruit cake you sent, you son of a bitch!"

"James, please—" I begged.

"It's ok, Daddy. I'm leaving… But I wanted all you people to know that the fruit of this man's loins is a flaming homo who's about to adopt a beautiful baby girl from China. And I'm going to love her for whomever she turns out to be, no matter what."

He was tearing up.

"You're the god damn devil, Daddy. You'll be elected President when hell freezes over."

"Well you better start color coordinating winter wear then, you freak! You hear me?!"

He put his sparkly glasses back on and dismissed me with a wave of the hand as he walked out, rainbow scarf trailing behind him.

We were about to start filming for the Depends diaper commercial.

"Where should we go for lunch after this?" I asked.

"BOMB THEM!" John M— shouted.

"No John, where do you want to eat?"

"ARM THE REBELS!"

"Seriously, do you feel like Chinese? Italian?"

"LEADING FROM BEHIND!"

"You've lost your mind, haven't you?"

"EXCEPTIONALISM!"

"That's what I thought," I sighed.

I sat in the Fox News studio, getting mic'd up for Sean H—'s show.

"It's good to see you, Sean," I said, leaning across the table to shake the man's hand. "How have you been?"

"I'm well, Governor," he said, slurring slightly. "The girl's family is no longer pressing charges. We were able to settle the matter under the table."

A pretty young intern brought him a glass of water and he took a sip as she turned to leave.

"Denise," he said, stopping her. "This is supposed to have children's tears in it. You just put a dash of salt in, didn't you? You honestly think I can't tell the difference?"

"I'm sorry, I—"

He threw the water in her face.

"Get out of here. You're fired."

She ran off crying as Sean turned back to me.

"I'll tell you Governor, I've got a hemorrhoid on my ass the size of a cherry. Been calling it Ed Schultz, cause it sort of looks like him... Fits right in with my twin genital warts, Chris Hayes and Rachel Maddow."

"Jesus, Sean. Sounds like you're coming apart at the seams."

"Oh well, you know," he said, removing a flask from his jacket pocket. "When you're wife's fucking Russell Brand out of spite, you've caught a new strain of treatment resistant gonorrhea, and you haven't shit in a week because it hurts too much, well... well... I don't even know what the fuck I'm saying... The moral of the story is: I'm full of shit, Governor. Literally full of shit."

"God will see you through it, Sean."

"Sure," he said, and downed the contents of the flask.

Now visibly drunk, he began the program.

"Good evening and welcome to the H— show, I'm your host, Sean H—. Tonight we'll be discussing the liberal climate change hoax and how it is really King Obama's plot to flood the United States with illegal immigrants and... and my teleprompter isn't working apparently... someone will be fired for that. Steve, I'm looking in your direction, Steve... Anyway, where was I? Oh yes, liberal climate change plot to secure the Hispanic vote and it all circles back to Hamas somehow and Emperor Obama's plot to overthrow Israel using the IRS... and Benghazi was staged in order to distract from Czar Obama's homosexual relationship with Eric Holder... It's all tied together."

The token liberal climate scientist was brought out like a lamb to the slaughter.

"Is climate change real?" Sean demanded.

"I believe the science is pretty conclusive—"

"So you're saying there is no God."

"Actually that's not what I'm saying at all—"

"So what you're saying is that God would allow his children to die. That God is making the world warmer on purpose!"

"God doesn't actually come into it—"

"You see!" Sean shouted. "From his own mouth: 'God doesn't come into IT'. What is that, some new liberal jive? I suppose we'll be seeing that hashtag everywhere for the next week and a half."

"I don't know what you're trying to—"

"No! Shut up!" Sean spat, fuming, veins popping out of his neck. "I am so sick of you liberal know-it-alls pretending you're all so much smarter than the rest of us. Well you know what?! You're not! So there!"

The guest shrugged into the camera.

"You get the hell out of my studio, you godless shit!" Sean shrieked. He then vomited on his desk, a small puddle of whiskey and a handful of half digested Combos. At the same moment his bowels let go with a wet rip, his pants filling with feces.

I slid back from the table. The stench was overpowering.

"Someone call me a cab," he whimpered, wiping his mouth with a handful of talking points. "I can't drive. They took my license away."

"We'll talk later, Sean," I said, getting up.

"Don't leave, Governor," I heard him beg as I walked away. "God, I'm so lonely."

A producer stopped me on my way out of the studio.

"Don't be embarrassed, Governor Huckleberry. He does this all the time. It's why we don't do the show live anymore."

Ann C—'s Adam's apple is much bigger in person. I mean really, it's *pronounced*. It was hard to follow what she was saying across the pre-CPAC conference table with that thing bouncing around.

What I didn't miss however was that something beneath the table was rubbing against my crotch with terrible persistence. I peered underneath to find a massive, stockinged foot, toenails yellow and ingrown, massaging me with a mounting rhythm.

I tried to swat the damn thing away, but Ann just smiled at me across the table, giving me a wink followed by a nasty tongue motion.

This went on for about an hour before the meeting let out.

I was able to avoid her in the hallway outside the conference room, but failed to make it to the first available elevator in time.

Desperate to get away, I took the stairs.

I made it to the ground floor, but got turned around there, coming out in a back alleyway. Nick was waiting with the car on the other side of the building.

Gathering my nerve, I set off down the passage at a quick pace.

I had almost reached the street when I heard the sound of clacking heels approaching behind me. Before I could turn to face my pursuer, I found myself pinned against the side of the building, my face shoved against the brickwork.

The deep voice boomed with terrible certainty.

"Oh God, I've wanted this for so long!"

"Ann!" I cried. "What are you doing?"

"I'm going to nail every Republican Presidential hopeful, Huckleberry! Starting with the oldest!"

"No means no!" I shouted, but she just laughed bitterly, saliva filming my ear.

"Spread 'em, Grandpa!"

She'd pulled down my pants and diaper and I could feel her trying to enter me.

"Don't! I have a spastic colon!"

"Struggle all you want. It's better that way."

I screamed.

"I thought you said pheasant hunting, Dick!" I shouted, standing over the dead homeless woman.

Dick C— laughed, reloading his smoking shotgun.

"No, you idiot, pheasants are out of season. I clearly said peasants! Quick and cunning—the deadliest game, Huckleberry!"

At that same moment a crack head leapt out of a patch of underbrush screaming, a pack of bloodhounds nipping at his heels. Dick dropped the man with one shot, the dogs tearing into him.

"God, don't you love this spring air?"

"Very refreshing," I agreed.

"So, Mike," Dick said, training his rifle on a young crippled boy whose wheelchair had become stuck in the mud. "I hear you're thinking of taking a run at the White House."

He pulled the trigger, half of Tiny Tim's head disappearing in a spray of gore.

"Doesn't this stuff bother you at all, Dick?"

"What stuff?" he asked, reloading.

"The killing people for sport stuff."

He looked at me like I was insane.

"Mike, I besmirched the memory of three thousand dead Americans to start a war under false pretenses for black goo they pump out of the ground. Gotta remember who you're talking to."

"Where do you get them?" I asked, motioning to the senior citizen crawling rather un-stealthily across a field on all fours.

"Free range," Dick said, leveling his shotgun. "Secret Service rounds them up for me. They replenish the preserve every couple of weeks... Damn things are everywhere these days."

"A little to your left," George B— said, motioning to me from his easel.

"Like this?" I asked, shifting position on the stool.

"Perfect. I want the light to catch your buttocks at the perfect angle."

I looked about the art studio. A large pastel drawing in the corner depicted a grinning Vladimir Putin receiving fellatio from Barack Obama against the backdrop of a burning Washington DC. Beside this sat a long line of dog portraits, several erotic sketches of Condoleezza R—, and an oil painting featuring Donald R— and Paul W— grappling over the ring of power in the belly of Mount Doom.

"I'm thinking of running for President, George," I said. "I was wondering if you had any advice for me. You seem like a pretty grounded guy."

He laughed. "Yeah, well maybe now. But when I was President I honestly thought I was losing my shit. You never get a moment's rest, Mike. It's all 'the country is under attack' this, and 'the economy is failing' that... blah blah blah blah... I'd be lying if I said it wasn't a crash course in insanity, and with one hell of a steep learning curve. Hell, never mind the policy decisions; I used to get lost in the White House. You know how many fuckin' rooms there are in that place?"

"I have no idea."

"The answer is too many, Mike," he said, shaking his head. "Way too fuckin' many."

"Governor Huckleberry!" a voice shouted from behind me.

I turned to face a disheveled homeless man approaching from across the street.

His beard was a matted mess, full of crusted globs of old food, his blue eyes wild and glazed over, his tin-foil hat shining in the noon day sun.

He hugged me before I could stop him, embracing me like an old lover.

"Thank God!" he cried, tears flowing.

"Please don't hurt me," I pleaded.

He pulled back and fixed me with his gaze.

"Don't you recognize me, Huckleberry?"

I looked for a way to slip him, perhaps find a police officer.

"It's me!" he sobbed. "It's Glenn B—!"

And by God, it was. I took him by the shoulders.

"Jesus Glenn, what are you doing out here?"

"Have to keep moving," he said, scratching at a scabby, scarred-over patch on his neck. "Can't stay indoors, no, that's how they get you."

"Who do you mean? Who are *they*?"

"Obama's men, of course," he said, scratching more vigorously, opening the wound further. He had similar injuries on his arms and legs.

"My God Glenn, what have you done to yourself?"

"Oh," he laughed, still scratching. "The microchips. I have to dig the microchips out. They implant them when I fall asleep, the bastards."

"Let me buy you some food, Glenn. When's the last time you ate?"

"You fool!" he shouted. "They put mind control drugs in the food! Are you trying to get me killed? I have to stay off the grid!"

"Of course, of course," I said, trying to calm him.

He pulled me in close then, eyes bulging.

"Who sent you? It was Beyoncé and Jay-Z wasn't it? Liberal puppet masters! Well I've got them pegged now!"

He took a long pull from what appeared to be a bottle of anti-freeze.

"Glenn, let me get you some help—"

"Don't trust anyone, Huckleberry!" he screamed, and then ran down the street flapping his arms like a bird.

"I'm not saying these people are parasites. Hell, even parasites eventually shrivel up and die. I'm just saying they're an awful burden on our system. We're a nation of laws, mind you, unlike whatever godless hellhole vomited *them* up."

The Texas crowd roared in approval.

"Now are you going to let them come in here and take your jobs, bringin' Ebola and Bubonic Plague and Small Pox and locusts and chupacabras!"

"What's a chupacabra?" someone shouted.

"That would be the South American cousin of the traditional Asiatic Gremlin."

"That sounds horrible!"

"Well it should," I affirmed.

"Sir," Nick said, pulling me aside. "Expanding the tent,

remember? Widening the base."

"Nick," I said, patting him on the shoulder. "Does this look like an 'expanding the tent' crowd to you?"

He looked around, the Gadsden flags riding high on the wind, the pitchforks raised, Mexican effigies burning. Nearby, a group of children broke open a piñata full of handcuffs. Gunmetal gleamed under the scorching sun.

"I suppose not, sir."

"You're damn right," I said quietly, looking to the south. "Now where the hell is Rick P—? He said he'd be here."

"His people said he wanted to make some sort of grand entrance, sir. He may be running for the nomination himself."

At that very instant a tank rolled over a hill to east, the man himself atop it, dressed in army fatigues.

The crowd began to cheer wildly at the sight, but as he neared it became apparent that something was wrong.

I could hear him shouting above the roar of the tank treads.

"I don't know how to steer this damn thing! Help! Someone help!"

People began to trample each other, scrambling to get out of the way, tripping over themselves.

The tank ran over about a quarter of the crowd, leaving a trail of crushed corpses in its wake.

I watched speechless as Rick P— and the tank kicked up dust

rolling on toward the Rio Grande, and eventually into it.

"I heard Michele B— is supposed to be here today. I always wanted to meet her," I said, leaning back in the limo seat.

"She's less interesting in person," Reince P— said, applying blush to his pale, clammy face.

"Why do you say that?"

"Because she's not a real person, Mike. The RNC paid Dade Robotics a few million bucks for her. We should get our money back if you ask me; all the damn thing does is malfunction."

"You're saying she's a robot?"

"Yeah, her and that Christine 'I'm not a witch' chick... Actually creeps me out a bit," Reince said, staring off into space. "It's like the Stepford Wives."

We sat in silence until the car rolled to a stop before the convention center.

We were escorted inside by security, a particularly sweaty bald man sticking to Reince like glue.

"Sir, she's been glitching all morning."

"How so?"

"It's her rhetoric chip, she keeps mixing things up. She wants to ban illegal immigrants from getting married and deport gays to South America."

"Jesus. Where is she now?"

"We were able to get her into a closed off staging area away from the public."

"Good. Take me there. Come along, Mike."

We entered a large store room full of various equipment, light rigging, rows upon rows of foldout chairs. Toward the back stood a group of security guards in a circle around Michele B—.

"How are we today, Michele?" Reince asked, motioning for the guards to step aside.

Her head spun around like the little girl's from *The Exorcist*, insane smile spread from ear to ear.

"Your mother's in here with us, Reince. Would you like to leave a message?"

"Very amusing. Now, when was the last time you came in for programming?"

Her mouth opened like a nutcracker's and "Blue Moon" by Bobby Vinton began to ring out, echoing through the room.

"Blue mooooooon, I saw you standing alone

Without a dream in my heart, without a love of my own.

Blue moooooooon…"

"That's what I thought," Reince said, turning to me. "She's completely lost it." He produced a remote control from his jacket pocket and hit the red kill switch, pointing it in her direction.

Nothing happened.

"Come on dammit," he pounded the switch, but to no effect.

Her expression shifted from one of whimsical mirth to one of unbridled hatred, her voice card beginning to glitch and distort.

"Hurricanes are messages from God. Women should be submissive, for they are of Adam's—Adam's—Adam's rib! Mi— Mi—Mi—minimum waaaaaaaaaaage is the Devil! The Devil King Obama, Osama, Obama, Osama! Un—Un—Un—Un-American Activities Committeeeeeeeeeeeeeeeeee!"

She grabbed two security guards by the hair and rammed their heads together, killing them instantly.

"Oh God!" Reince shouted. "She's gone homicidal! Run Mike, run for your life!"

I tripped, scrambling backwards on my hands away from her. She laughed, a horrible metallic, inhuman cackle as the other guards piled on top of her, one of them finally able to cut her power manually.

"Intellectual movement at its core, intellectual movement at its core, intellectuallll moooooovemeeent attt itttttsss coooooorrrrrrrrreeeeeeeeee—" her voice faded, dropping low as the artificial life drained from her. Sparks and smoke shot from her eyes, the smell of burnt plastic filling the air.

"Damn that was close," Reince said, helping me to my feet. "You all right, Governor?"

"I think so," I said, dusting myself off.

I looked over to the smoldering, melted heap of what was Michele B—.

"Well, I guess that's one less primary opponent."

"With one voice we must shout it from the rooftops: Don't tread on me!"

The crowd at the Cliven B— ranch roared with approval, raising their assorted firearms into the midday sun, cellulite filled, flabby arms giggling, gizzard necks puffing with pride, stained wife-beaters and Hooters t-shirts soaked through with sweat.

Cliven himself took my hand as I stepped off the stage, his voice churning like so much gravel. I could only make out a few words here and there.

"Yer a… true 'murican… God damn… and sandbaggin'… black helicopters… niggers off my… blood moon… come on down here…'murica… rise up!"

I patted him on the shoulder.

"My thoughts exactly, Cliven."

"Pooped my pants," he added, grinning as if it was our little secret.

"Well," I said, adjusting my tie, "I certainly know how that feels."

I had to wade through a sea of militiamen to get back to the car, but a nice young man was kind enough to escort me through the crowd.

"What's your name, son?"

"Jerad," he said, adjusting his camouflage cap. "Jerad Miller, Gov. Huckleberry."

"Well it's a pleasure to meet you, Jerad. I'm glad to see upstanding patriotic youth standing up against tyranny."

"Thank you, Governor. I just hope things don't get violent out here. That would be a tragedy."

"Nonsense," I laughed, waving him off. "The tree of liberty must be refreshed from time to time with the blood of patriots and tyrants. Thomas Jefferson said that." I was getting into the car then. "Assert yourself, Jerad. Revolution starts with the individual."

He seemed lost in thought as I shut the door.

"What a nice young man," I remarked to Nick as we pulled away.

"Ever noticed how when Al Sharpton says my name it comes out sounding like Lumbar? Rush Lumbar. Old coon's going senile. You'd think Helen Keller was running his teleprompter." His laughter rang out through the cigar smoke filled haze of the limousine. "What's he yammering on about now anyway? Another junior scholar get shot?"

He exploded in laughter again.

"Not sure, Rush," I said, cracking a window, the atmosphere clearing a bit.

He was in the process of crushing up Oxycontin on a small mirror with the back of a lighter.

"Not that I have anything against the dark meat," he continued. "Hell, the best piece of ass I ever had was as black as a moonless midnight. Man, did I tear that shit up! We were role playing, you see

– master and slave. You can guess who was who." He howled with laughter again, elbowing me in the ribs. "You like the brown sugar, Huckleberry? Come on, you can tell old Rushbo. I bet you do. I bet you spray 'em down like a Mississippi fire hose, you dog!"

I turned to Jesus, who was bringing a martini to his lips.

"Nice friend you've got there, Mike. Really fits your wholesome image."

In two long snorts, Rush took up most of the powder, throwing his head back with a flourish.

"Oh, oh man, that's the medicine! First class ticket to numbsville! Drip! Drip! Drippppp!"

Red and blue flashers popped up behind us.

I turned to see a police cruiser riding our tail.

"Shit!" Rush shouted, sucking up the rest of the powder like a Hoover vacuum.

He pulled a bag out of his pocket, a tennis ball sized bundle of assorted pills.

"I don't have prescriptions for these, Huckleberry," he said nervously. "So here's what's going to happen. You're going to hide these up your ass."

"No way," I said, waving him off.

"Yes way," he said, creeping towards me. "If I go to jail I'm going to make your life a living hell when I get out. I'll make it my fucking mission to ruin you, Huckleberry. Now get this up your shithole!"

It was easier than I thought.

Ann C— had really loosened me up.

"Well, if Rand could pull his tongue out of Cory Booker's ass for a minute, Governor Huckleberry would love to speak with him."

Nick hung up abruptly and turned to me.

"We'll catch him one of these days, sir. He can't ignore us much longer, or else we'll expose him for the liberal sleeper he is."

"Good," I said, looking around the waiting room in the New Jersey Governor's office.

A man walked up to us.

"Governor Huckleberry, Governor C— will see you now."

"Wonderful. You wait here, Nick. Don't think this will be long."

The man led me down a long hallway to a large door at its end. He then turned to face me.

"Have you been here before?"

"No," I said.

"Alright, well we have a few simple rules for the purpose of safety."

"Are you serious?"

Ignoring my question, the man continued.

"He's been in hiding since the bridge scandal, and he's developed a slight photosensitivity, so we keep the lighting very low. He'll be behind his desk. Please stay out of grabbing range." He handed me a bag of McDonalds hamburgers. "There are seven Big Macs in here. It should be enough to keep him sated during your meeting. You are to slide them across the desk, and once again I must warn you not to get too close. Anything in grabbing distance you're going to lose."

"You must be joking," I laughed.

His expression flat, the man raised his left hand, which was missing both the index and middle fingers.

"That look funny to you?"

I swallowed hard, shaking my head.

In the darkness of the office I sat down opposite the hulking mass, sliding a burger across the desk.

C— leaned over the offering, throwing a shroud over his head.

"Don't look at me!"

I turned to face the wall, only then noticing the crude finger painted murals of ketchup and mustard that covered most of the room like primitive cave drawings. It was hard to keep my vision averted however with the awful inhuman slurping noises emanating from beneath the shroud.

At length they subsided, C— removing the cover.

"What the hell do you want Huckleberry?"

"What I want is your assurance that you won't run for President. If you do this you will move to the top of my list for Vice Presidential picks."

His eyes moved to the bag of burgers.

"Give me another one of those while I mull it over."

I slid two across the desk as a sign of my good will, and on came the shroud again, along with the terrible slurping sounds.

"All right, Huckleberry," he said when he'd finished. "You've got yourself a deal." He leaned forward out of the darkness, a tidal wave of undulating chins. "Shake on it?" He smiled, his teeth looking sharp.

"That won't be necessary," I said, standing.

I slid the bag of burgers across the desk, and this time he tore into them without the cover of the shroud, the horrible, guttural sounds following me out of the darkened office.

"How did it go?" Nick asked as we left the building.

"Fine," I said. "But cancel lunch, Nick. I can't eat just now."

"Let me show you something, Governor," Wayne L— said as we waited off stage at the NRA rally. "Everyone wonders why I'm such an asshole. Well here, let me show you why."

He dropped his trousers.

"I tried jerking off with a pair of tweezers once, almost tore the damn thing clean off. I have to tell my wife when it's in."

"Jesus Wayne, put that thing away.

"Her words *exactly*."

The crowd was getting wound up, I could hear them.

"Wayne, what sort of an event is this again? This an open carry crowd?"

"Sort of," he said, peeking out through the curtain. "This is open carry for the mentally disabled."

"Mentally disabled?"

He grew serious. "Governor, surely you're not suggesting that we overlook the second amendment rights of the mentally disabled. They make up half the Republican base, after all."

"Whatever," I said, turning to walk out.

"Oh and Governor," Wayne called after me. "Most of them are already packing. So try not to get them too riled up."

Later, at the hospital, as a doctor was removing the buckshot from my ass, I turned to Nick with tears in my eyes.

"Do you think I'm being punished for something?"

He put a hand on my shoulder.

"Maybe we all are, sir."

Jesus popped up and took a Polaroid of my ass.

"Oh yes," he said, waving the ejected photo as it developed. "That, Mike, is a thing of beauty."

I began to weep openly.

"Oh don't be such a baby, Mike," Jesus laughed. "Come talk to me when you've been scourged, crucified, and stabbed in the friggin' guts with a spear, you pansy."

"Forget herding cats, that's not the right metaphor at all. Cats are intelligent," House Speaker John B— whined from beneath the glow of the tanning bed. "At least they have some innate sense of self preservation. No, it's more like rounding up escaped mental patients. Some are just walking in circles, some are crawling up trees, and some are on a mad dash to Jodie Foster's house... Ted C— has more influence in the House than I do, Huckleberry, and that greasy faggot is nuttier than a squirrel turd. I mean it. I'm not religious, but I swear that man is the fucking anti-Christ."

He sat up and took a swig of red wine, sticking a Camel Ultra Light between his lips.

"You don't have to tell me, John," I said, lighting it for him. "Can I count on your support then, for my run?"

He nodded. "Of course."

"Good," I smiled. "Now, a little bird told me that you may have some leverage on Ted C— that you've been sitting on. Did I hear correctly?"

A grin spread across his leathery, pumpkin hued face.

"Oh yes."

The photos were older, but of a good quality.

They clearly depicted a young Rafael Edward C— placing first in a Drag Queen competition.

I knew that smirk anywhere, even underneath the heavy makeup and curled ringlets of dark hair.

His back was arched to accentuate his padded bosom, and he was in the act of blowing a kiss off a bejeweled hand as the crown was set atop his sparkling head.

"This will do nicely," I said, grinning.

"Governor," Nick spoke as we waited for a limo in the hotel lobby, "did you by any chance hire a group of men to don blackface and incite riots during the Ferguson, Missouri protests?"

"Yes, Nick. I did."

"Why in God's name would you do that?"

"Bill O— bet me five hundred bucks that I didn't have the stones to go through with it." I grinned. "Never bet against a man who can shit himself while keeping a straight face, Nick."

"I'll try to remember that, Governor."

He was silent for a moment. "Have you ever shit yourself while I was in the room, sir?"

"Just did, my good man," I said, removing a cheap cigar from its bloodstained packaging and running it under my nose.

It smelled like victory.

Ted C— patted Mike L—'s head as we sat at the table in Tortilla Coast, Mike's tongue lolling from his mouth, saliva dribbling down his chin.

"Nice pet you have there, Ted," I said, opening the menu.

Ted leaned back in his chair.

"He's dumb, but loyal. Isn't that right, Mikey?"

Mike L— clapped his hands together and rocked back and forth chuckling, excited by the sound of his own name.

A waitress came over to take our order.

"Mike will have a grilled cheese sandwich on white bread, no crusts," Ted spoke. "I will have the steak fajitas."

"I'll just have a Diet Coke," I said. "I won't be staying long."

The waitress left and we got down to business.

I slid a manila envelope across the table and Ted examined its contents.

"Have you shown these to anyone else?" he asked, sweat breaking out on his brow.

"No, but there are copies in several safety deposit boxes to be opened should anything happen to me."

"Smart. Well, what do you want from me then?"

"Just your blind allegiance. You're *my* attack dog now. Your policy will suit my interests. And put all notions of running for President out of mind."

Mike L— growled, baring his teeth.

"Easy boy," Ted whispered, scratching behind Mike's ear, the man settling. "And if I should refuse?"

"Then these pictures will be sent to every major media outlet in the country, Ted. Oh, may I call you Ted? Or do you prefer Miss Luscious Cubana?"

"Ted will be fine," he said, lowering his head in submission.

"Today, Blacks and Hispanics make up about fifty-eight percent of the US prison population, despite making up only about a quarter of the overall population. A majority of those incarcerated are in prison for committing crimes against members of their own race. If that's not a cultural problem, I don't know what is," Bill O— grumbled into the camera. "Now Eric Holder has ordered yet another autopsy on the body of Michael Brown, just another example of this administration's overreach into matters of state. I wonder what they'll discover this go round? Let me spare you the suspense—he's still a soulless degenerate punk who got just what was coming to him. Honestly, what was this thug going to amount to if he lived? That cop did us all a favor if you ask me. Hell, I wish I'd been there, I would have shot him myself!"

He shuffled the papers on his desk, collecting himself.

"Well that's it for our show, I'm Bill O—. Be sure to visit us online and pick up a copy of my new book: *Hey, You Don't Look Like Me!* Goodnight."

"And we're out," the studio director said.

"Great show, Bill," I said, walking over to shake his hand.

"Huckleberry, didn't see you there," he said, rising to greet me. "How are you?"

"Well Bill, and yourself?"

"Great. Just great. This Missouri thing has been fantastic for ratings. The base eats this shit up like hot cakes."

"That's what got me thinking, Bill. What do you say to producing a town hall style meeting with some well groomed, articulate African Americans to set the record straight on the cause of this mess?"

He nodded. "Yes, just like I've been saying—a cultural problem, not an institutional one. The degradation of the African American family unit. Lack of values. I love it, Huckleberry."

"And the fact that the community immediately took to violence afterward."

"Like animals, yes. All notion of due process forgotten. The façade of civility cast aside like a spent watermelon rind."

"Get a black audience to nod and say 'Amen' and 'Hallelujah' to all that and your ratings will go through the roof."

"And I assume you'll help me moderate it?"

"Naturally," I smiled.

"And what if we can't find blacks to agree with us?"

"Then you just scoop some off the street, dress them up, give them some cue cards and pay them in malt liquor. Do I have to think of everything?"

He laughed. "You're the devil, Huckleberry. You know that?"

"No Bill, I'm just a messenger."

He laughed, putting his arm around me as we walked from the studio.

"I feel like celebrating. There's a Fox News staff party tonight if you feel like going. We throw them every month, get's pretty wild. At the last one I saw Megyn K— going down on Andrea T— and Michelle M— getting pissed on by Jenna L—. Was a thing of beauty, let me tell you... Sean H— was a shitshow, as usual. Threw up in a punch bowl... I caught Eric B— and Greg G— jerking each other off in a bathroom... Steve D— was doing nitrous and fell off a balcony, and Tucker C— was so high he showed up in nothing but a bowtie... Oh, and old Hammerkraut wears a merkin as it turns out."

"What the hell is a merkin?"

"Pubic wig," he answered, smiling. "So you wanna go or not?"

"No thanks, Bill," I said. "Maybe some other time."

"Suit yourself."

"It's really coming together, Dad," I said, leaning over the old man's bed. "We might actually have a shot at this thing."

"I always did like a tongue up the ass," he said, sucking on a juice box. "You ever had someone stick their tongue up your pooper, Steve?"

"It's Michael, Dad. And no, I can't say that I have."

He seemed disappointed by this. "Well, you're missing out. Get's me harder than a roll of quarters."

"Can we please just have a normal conversation for once?" I pleaded.

"You're too repressed, Steve. Sexuality is a big part of life. It's religious even—Godly."

"He's got a point there, Mike," Jesus spoke from the doorway.

"Oh just cram it for once, would you Jesus?"

"See," my father spoke, "you're so pent-up you're talking to imaginary friends."

I moved in closer then, taking his hand in my own.

"It's very important that I know you're with me on this, Dad. You're my father, and I want so much for you to be proud of me."

"I'm not your father, dammit! Some gypsies left you on the doorstep in the middle of the night. I wanted to drown you in a wash basin but Mae wouldn't let me, you curse of a bastard!"

As I stood there speechless a young nurse came in.

"It's time for your sponge bath, Mr. Huckleberry."

"Well it's about god damn time," my father said, sitting up. "I'm a very dirty boy."

"Breitbart was a pederast," Rick S— whispered to me at the conservative press gathering as a picture of the man himself came up on a large screen in tribute. "He and Matt D— used to fly to Thailand for cocaine fueled orgies with underage boys."

"That's horrifying," I said.

"It's the damn homosexuals, Huckleberry. They're infecting even the best of us with their sinful predilections. They must be stopped."

"That's what I wanted to speak with you about, Rick. Should I be elected President, would you consider heading up my cultural cleansing program? We need to exterminate these monsters, and something tells me you're just the man for the job."

"Governor," he said, placing a hand over his heart, "I thought you'd never ask."

"Governor Sarah P—," I said, extending my hand. "It's lovely to see you again."

"Wow, yah. Welcome to Alaska, Governor Huckleberry. It's such an honor to have you in my home. Please come in."

"Thank you," I said, moving into the house and removing my coat.

"This is my study," she said, leading me into a large room. A fire glowed in the hearth, illuminating the various stuffed and mounted animals that adorned the walls. The floor was littered with coloring books.

"Your children's," I said.

"No, those are mine," she corrected.

She pulled close to me suddenly, sliding a hand down my pants.

"Listen, Huckleberry, I didn't call you here today to make small talk. I'm getting into the White House one way or another. You need me to win over the Republican women's vote, so you're gonna marry me and take me with you to Washington."

"I don't think that's—"

"I betcha wonder what's underneath all these fancy clothes, dontcha?" she said, touching herself provocatively. "Yah, momma grizzly's gonna lay your wrinkled ass down by the fire!"

She jumped on top of me, pushing me back onto the bearskin rug before the hearth.

"You've got the wrong impression," I tried to say, my eyes rolling back in my head as she grinded against my crotch lustily. She tore off her clothes to reveal gleaming leather lingerie beneath.

"Yah," she spat, between heavy breaths, dry humping away. "I betcha you're a real freak, aren'tcha Huckleberry?!"

"No, I'm rather conventional actually," I groaned, closing my eyes, lost in our motion, the heat of our friction.

She'd taped my mouth shut before I even knew what was happening, and by the time I realized it, my hands and feet were bound in fuzzy handcuffs.

"Yah," she said, producing a black riding crop. "I betcha like to get the shit beaten out of you! Dontcha?!"

I shook my head furiously, producing the most disapproving sounds I could muster.

"That's what they all say," she laughed, standing and stepping on my crotch with a high heel.

Tears streamed down my face as I fought against the restraints.

"Mistress Sarah doesn't believe in safe words!" she shouted. "Now let us begin!"

"So, who here blames President Obama for the death of young Michael Brown?" I asked the room of well groomed African Americans.

About seventy-five percent of the audience raised their hands, as they'd been instructed to do.

"Let's hear some opinions on it," Bill O— said, taking over.

A particularly jittery looking middle aged man—a heroin addict we picked up in Harlem—raised a shaky hand.

"You have the floor, sir," Bill said.

"Thank you," he spoke, his voice cracking, looking down at his script cards. "I believe that Barack Obama has abandoned black youth to the sway of drugs and rap music with his light handed, PC policies, and that the African American community as a whole would be better served by a heavy handed conservative administration; an administration unafraid of bringing the hammer down when necessary. I think we need some tough love." He looked up from his cards, seemingly pleased with his performance. "Yo, do I get my money now? Scooby D gotta see a ho about a bag."

I turned to Bill.

"We can edit that out in post," he assured me.

I looked up to see Jesus dancing in the back row, wearing huge, blinged-out sunglasses and a golden clock on a diamond studded necklace, a forty of Colt 45 in one hand, a massive blunt in the other.

"Yeah Mike," he shouted, "You know what time it is!"

I spotted Rand P— coming out of a coffee shop, cramming a Danish into his stupid face. His eyes widened with panic as he saw me and Nick running towards him.

"Rand!" I shouted in full sprint. "You son of a bitch! You stay right there!"

He dropped the Danish and was off and running, weaving through traffic.

We lost sight of him down a narrow side street and so proceeded with caution.

"He's a squirrely little bastard. Don't let him get the jump on you," I whispered.

At that same moment, Rand leapt out of a garbage bin onto Nick's back. "Eeeeeeeiiiiiiiiiiiyyyyaaaaahhhhhhh!" he shrieked before sinking his teeth into Nick's shoulder.

"Get him off!" Nick squealed. "Get him off! Get him off!"

I punched Rand in the back of the head, at which point he released his grip on Nick, falling backward.

I hit him in the face several times, bloodying his nose.

"Why have you been ducking my calls, Rand? I've been trying to get in touch with you for months. You too good to talk to the former Governor of Arkansas?!"

"It was Ted," he gasped, blood running down his face. "Ted said I wasn't supposed to talk to you. And his word is law, Huckleberry. Even you know that." He pinched his nose, stemming the flow of blood.

"Things are working a bit differently now, Rand. Ted is in my pocket, so either you are as well, or I'm gonna run you and your whole shifty, flip floppin' family out of American politics. You get me?"

"The Republican nomination is mine, Huckleberry!"

I sighed. "Suit yourself. But know this, little boy: come debate time, you better bring something more than cribbed Wikipedia entries."

I turned to Nick who was bleeding profusely from his shoulder.

"Come along, Nick. Let's get you patched up."

"This Jessa girl is such a pouty slut," I said between bong hits.

It had occurred to me that in order to tap into the mindset of young voters Nick and I should get high and watch late night television. "I rather like that Marnie, though. She's the only one on this show with any class."

"That's Brian Williams's daughter."

"No shit? How about that."

"Yeah, and the one with the shag carpet eyebrows and resting bitch face, that's David Mamet's daughter."

"Now that you mention it, I do see the resemblance."

"I just don't understand why Lena Dunham is naked all the time. It's like 'sweetie, *no one* wants to see that,'" Nick said through a mouthful of Cheetos.

"Right?" I said. "Now that you mention it, this show is making me feel a little sick. All the self pity and nervous shifting. It paints young women as adrift and emotionally immature."

"Well, it is a comedy, sir."

"More like psychological horror. This is the future of our country, Nick. Don't tell me you find that comforting."

He sat up with a flash of visible paranoia.

"You're right, let's watch something else."

He switched to Cartoon Network, where we watched a show about a boy and his magical talking dog fighting some sort of ice wizard, followed by something called *Superjail!* and several episodes of something called *China, IL.*

Needless to say, we didn't learn much.

"Sir, do you think this is wise?" Nick shouted above the roar of the plane's engine.

"Jesus put himself amongst the sinners, Nick. Amongst the unclean, the corrupt, the morally bankrupt. That is where the work is to be done... Now you're absolutely certain that this Justin Beaver is popular among the twenty-somethings?"

"I believe so, sir," Nick answered.

"This is by far the most ill conceived idea you're ever had, Mike," Jesus said as we looked down at the bustling concert crowd.

I didn't acknowledge him; I just pulled my goggles on and made sure my parachute was secure.

And then I was falling, the crowd growing closer and closer, whirling up beneath me. I pulled the ripcord, the canopy opening with a strong jerk.

Soaring over the crowd, the Beaver fans gazing up in rapturous wonder, I admit that for a moment I felt godlike, with all the world's eyes upon me.

This feeling faded quickly however as I approached the stage at a much greater speed than I had anticipated.

Musicians scattering, I connected with a terrible crash, but somehow miraculously unhurt.

Untangling myself from the parachute, I quickly recovered, spinning around and raising my arms to the crowd to receive their adoration.

Mike Huckleberry.

Hip dude.

Happening cat.

Totally viable candidate for President.

A kid with absurdly tight jeans shuffled up to me from off stage holding a bass guitar in one hand, pointing accusingly with the other.

"Dude, you totally crushed Justin!"

"Yeah," I shouted, giving him two thumbs up. "Totally crushing, dude! I'm hip to your youthful lingo!"

"No!" he said, pointing to my parachute. "You killed him!"

I lifted the parachute from where I'd landed, and beneath it was indeed the mangled, lifeless form of Justin Beaver—revered songster of the American youth.

"Fuck me," I whispered.

I was at my wit's end.

Nothing seemed as it should, and I felt as if the world entire was conspiring against me.

So many gaffes and blunders.

My poll numbers were tanking nationwide, even with the unexpected boost I got from killing Justin Beaver.

I took to isolation on my estate, physically ill with the thought of losing the nomination. I couldn't eat. I couldn't sleep.

Huckleberry the joke, they said.

Huckleberry the has-been.

Huckleberry the failure.

I was a man haunted, letting my nails and hair grow long and unkempt, collecting my urine in mason jars and storing them with obsessive care.

Ronald Reagan came to me every night in my dreams dressed like Julius Caesar, blood running from his many stab wounds, pointing at me accusingly.

"ET TU, HUCKLEBERRY? ET TUUUUUUUUUUUUUU?!"

I always woke with a massive erection.

What did *that* mean?

Nick would speak to me through my locked bedroom door, offering words of comfort, and I would cling to them with the same desperate intensity as a man adrift would a life preserver.

Until one night a note was slipped under the door.

It read simply:

"Sir, I know how to salvage the campaign. Clean yourself up. We leave for Kansas in the morning. – Nick."

"Nick," I said, guiding the giraffe along on its leash. "This seems somewhat satanic, don't you think?"

Nick laughed.

"This is well beyond Satan, sir."

We'd been walking for what felt like hours through the foggy Kansas countryside, and I was beginning to grow weary.

"Almost there, sir," Nick assured.

And before I knew it, from out the fog there appeared two massive grinning statues bearing the likenesses of Charles and David K—.

Before them lay a sacrificial altar rife with slain animal carcasses in various stages of decay.

I pulled the giraffe up alongside it.

"I'm not sure I can go through with this, Nick," I said, tears welling in my eyes. "I always liked giraffes."

"Sir," Nick spoke, producing a long knife from his coat pocket, "you need the blessing of the K— brothers if you want to be President. This is the only way. The larger and more exotic the sacrifice, the better." He handed me the knife. "Now, do you remember the incantation?"

I nodded sadly, turning toward the statues and bowing my head.

"Lop har kommet, shivun-tuk somnia."

"Again," Nick said.

"Lop har kommet, shivun-tuk somnia."

"Again, sir—louder."

"Lop har kommet, shivun-tuk somnia!"

"Louder!"

"LOP HAR KOMMET, SHIVUN-TUK SOMNIA!"

Lightning flashed and thunder boomed, the K— statues' eyes taking on a blue luminance.

"Now sir," Nick urged.

"I'm am so sorry," I said to the giraffe.

I then opened its throat, turning away as the animal collapsed in a heap on the altar.

The deed was done.

Following my sacrifice to the K— brothers, events turned in my favor in rapid succession.

Video surfaced of Mitt R— and his former running mate Paul R— in mid-coitus on top of a pile of money.

Marco R— choked to death on a chimichanga while being ambushed by Dreamers at a lunch counter.

Doctor Ben C— was sentenced to thirty years in prison for having been found to have conducted over four hundred brain surgeries while under the influence of various prescription pain medications.

In response to her continued coverage of his Wikipedia plagiarism, Rand P— challenged Rachel Maddow to a duel on national television. She accepted—old timey pistols at dawn on the banks of the Potomac... Rand's pistol jammed and Maddow blew off his nutsack in front of a crowd.

He retreated from politics in shame.

Herman C— was committed to a mental institution after being found wandering the streets of McDonough, Georgia in a suit of pizza boxes shouting "Nine-Nine-Nine!" at passersby.

Newt G— was stabbed to death by a conspiratorial group of scorned women.

The dregs of the field submitted to the inevitability of my nomination, and I soon found myself running unopposed.

We were attending a production of *A Streetcar Named Desire*, featuring Senator Lindsey G— in the role of Blanche DuBois, celebrating my upcoming nomination. I leaned back and put my arm around Sarah P—, now my fiancée. "I'm not wearing any panties," she whispered, her breath hot against my neck. Her hand moved to my crotch, massaging, and I groaned aloud.

Between the lilting, beautifully cadenced drawl of Lindsey's voice proclaiming that he'd "always relied upon the kindness of strangers," and Sarah whispering obscenities in my ear, I did not hear the creaking of the box door opening behind us, nor the soft clicking of high heels approaching.

By the grace of God, my assailant tripped, falling forward, and the bullet that was meant for the back of my skull hit me in the ass instead.

I leapt up, turning to face a heavily made up Ted C— rising from the darkness with a revolver.

I grabbed his gun hand, trying to wrestle the weapon from him.

"Ted! What the hell do you think you're doing?!"

"It's Miss Luscious Cubana! Always has been, always will be!" he shrieked. "And if I can't be President, then neither will you!"

Sarah bit into his leg and he screamed, dropping the gun. He looked about for a moment, panicked, then leapt from the balcony to the stage, twisting his ankle and stopping the show.

"Sic semper tyrannis!" he shouted, pointing up toward our box.

He then attempted to make good his escape, but lost his balance and fell into the orchestra pit, breaking his neck.

"Are you all right, my darling?" Sarah asked, rushing to my side.

"I think so," I said, applying pressure to my wounded ass.

"That was close, Mike," Jesus said, stepping out from the shadows of our viewing box.

"Yeah, a little heads up would have been nice."

"But that was your final test, Mike," Jesus said, beaming. "And you passed with flying colors." He put his hand on my shoulder. "You're ready now."

They had to wheel Chris C— onto the RNC stage on the back of a flatbed truck to accept the Vice Presidential nomination.

"Thank you, this is such an honor," he spoke through the wet, lapping jiggle of his massive jowls. He was a little breathy from the exertion, but he managed to pull off my introduction rather eloquently.

"Let's face it, ladies and gentlemen, you're not here tonight to stare at my ugly mug." He struggled briefly to motion to himself, unable to do so with his T-Rex arms.

The audience laughed anyway, humoring him.

"No, we're here for the man of the hour; a true blue, red blooded American; a man who wears his spiritual beliefs on his sleeve, and is unafraid to acknowledge their influence on his policy; a man who has faced down much adversity, and become the stronger for it; a man whose kindness and generosity seem to know no bounds. You all know who I'm talking about, let's hear it for him, the next President of the United States—Michael Dale Huckleberry!"

I stood from where I'd been praying backstage and turned to Jesus. He smiled, adjusting my tie.

"Look at you," he spoke, his voice full of pride. "Oh the places you'll go, Mike."

He kissed my forehead gently, turning me toward the stage, and I gazed through the curtains out at the cheering crowd. Some of them, the true believers, still held the old signs from the beginning of the campaign:

Mike Huckleberry for President.
Fucking the Future.

And I would.

God willing, I would fuck the shit out of it.

"Now go forth and conquer the earth in my name," Jesus whispered in my ear.

"Yes Lord," I said, and stepped out to meet my destiny.

About the Author

W.J. Renehan is the Editorial Director of Dark Hall Press, a publisher of first quality Horror and Science Fiction. His book *The Art of Darkness: Meditations on the Effect of Horror Fiction* is also available from New Street Communications, LLC. He is an alumnus of Dean College, SUNY New Paltz, and the University of Rhode Island.

ALSO OF INTEREST

FROM NEW STREET

Capsized: Jim Nalepka's Epic 119 Day Survival Voyage Aboard the Rose Noëlle
By Steven Callahan

"Soulful, emotional ... earnest and engrossing." – KIRKUS

Beast: A Slightly Irreverent Tale About Cancer (And Other Assorted Anecdotes)
By James Capuano

"A surprisingly life-affirming tale." - Susan Sarandon

Hemingway's Paris: Our Paris?
by H.R. Stoneback

" ... takes the reader inside the soul of Hemingway's Paris, penetrating the surface of guide-books." - A.E. Hotchner

Pink Elephants
by W.J. Renehan

"A political American Psycho." - Arthur Goldwag, critically-acclaimed author of The New Hate: A History of Fear and Loathing on the Populist Right

Teaching Salinger's Nine Stories
By Brad McDuffie

"Long overdue ... an innovative and invaluable resource." - Kenneth Slawenski, *author of* J. D. Salinger: A Life

CPSIA information can be obtained at www.ICGtesting.com
Printed in the USA
BVOW04s2150210115

384428BV00006B/58/P

9 780692 310892